The Lonely Penguin

Written and illustrated
by Petr Horáček

Collins

Crunch crunch! Who's coming through the snow?

It's Penguin. He's lonely.

Crunch crunch! Penguin's looking for his friends.

He can't think where they can be.

Crunch crunch! Penguin's running through the snow.

He's sliding on the frosty ice.

Crunch crunch!
Penguin's looking everywhere.

Penguin climbs up the hill.
Are his friends at the top?

No. Penguin looks down into the sea.
Are his friends at the bottom?
Penguin jumps into the air.

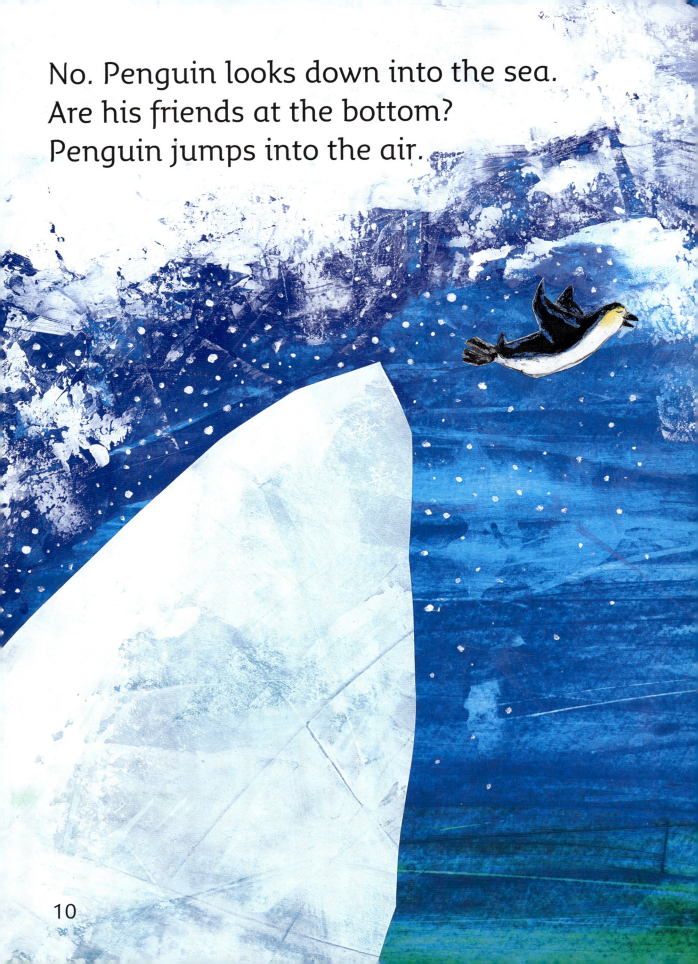

SPLASH!

Yes! Penguin finds his friends swimming in the cold water.

They all laugh and say,
"Where have you been?"

A story map

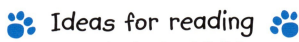

Ideas for reading

Written by Clare Dowdall, PhD
Lecturer and Primary Literacy Consultant

Learning objectives: recognise automatically an increasing number of familiar high frequency words; use syntax and context when reading for meaning; identify the main events and characters in stories; retell stories, ordering events using story language

Curriculum links: Citizenship: Taking part – developing skills of communication and participation; Geography: Where in the world is Barnaby Bear?

High frequency words: who, can't, where, be, down, laugh

Interest words: lonely, penguin, crunch, sliding, through, everywhere, climbs, friends

Word count: 93

Resources: flashcards of the tricky and high frequency words, paper and pens

Build a context for reading

- Ask children to share what they know about penguins. Look at the front cover together. Discuss where the penguin is and what the weather is like.

- Read the title and blurb with the children. Ask children to explain what it is like to feel lonely, giving examples from their experiences, and why Penguin might be lonely.

- Show children the tricky and high frequency words using flashcards. Help them to read the words.

Understand and apply reading strategies

- Walk through the book together. Ask children to describe what is happening in each picture.

- Model how to read pp2–3 aloud with expression, emphasising the repeated phrase "Crunch crunch!"

- Ask children to read the rest of the book in pairs. Remind them to help each other with tricky words and to use the pictures to help them read unfamiliar words.

- Listen to children as they read, praising them for using expression, attempting tricky words, and reading with fluency.